GNIT-WIT GNIPPER
AND THE
FEROCIOUS FIRE ANTS

Episode Two
of
The Misadventures of Gnipper the Gnome

WRITTEN BY
T.J. LANTZ

ILLUSTRATED BY
ANA SANTO

This book is a **ROSEHAVEN** adventure.
What exactly is Rosehaven?

Rosehaven is a multi-series Fantasy world, in which mythological creatures live in hiding on the outskirts of human exploration. It currently consists of three separate book series: Rosehaven, The Misadventures of Gnipper the Gnome, and The Dudley Diaries. Each of these series contains overlapping setting and characters, but differ in tone and reading level. The goal of Rosehaven is to offer young children an enjoyable fantasy world that grows with them as they become stronger readers. Currently Rosehaven offers:

The Misadventures of Gnipper the Gnome (For ages 7 and up, fully illustrated single sitting reads of about 50 pages. Each book is a standalone episode.):

This series tells the story of Gnipper Tallhat, a twelve year old gnome desperately trying to earn respect in her community for her scientific inventions. Unfortunately, everything she does seems to backfire.

Gnit-Wit Gnipper and the Perilous Plague
Gnit-Wit Gnipper and the Ferocious Fire-Ants
Gnit-Wit Gnipper and the Devious Dragon

The Dudley Diaries (For ages 9 and up, fully illustrated single sitting reads of about 50 pages. Each book is a standalone episode):

Follows the tales of Sir Dudley Tinklebutton, a knight of the Coalition of the Burning Heart. Sir Dudley isn't your typical heroic knight: he's scared of insects, he's never slain anything, and he's only chivalrous when he thinks he can get something out of it. Can Sir Dudley overcome his cowardly qualities to become the hero he needs to be?

Sir Dudley Tinklebutton and the Dragon's Lair
Sir Dudley Tinklebutton and the Sword of Cowardice
Sir Dudley Tinklebutton and the Unholy Grail

Rosehaven (For ages 10 and up. Novel Series, @ 300 pages each)

This tells the main story of the *retics*, creatures forced into hiding by a group of humans tasked with hunting them down. It follows the lives of several key figures: Jaxon the loud-mouthed demon who can control the elements, Tyranna the shape-shifter, learning to come to grips with her new world, and Reginald, a thousand year old Tree-ent knight dedicated to saving as many lives as he can. Together they must navigate conflicts in the human world, and in their own community, before war wipes the retics out forever.

Rise of the Retics (Book 1)
Return of the Fae-blood (Book 2)

"Back, you gigantic, winged menace!" Gnipper screamed the words as she swung the iron skillet she usually wore as a hat in a wide-arcing circle toward her assailant.

It hissed in return, but refused to back away.

"I said get away!" Gnipper snapped even louder. "I'm a gnome you stupid bug, not a snack!"

Gnipper had already retreated to the corner of her basement laboratory, away from any of the dangerous chemicals that might have helped her out of this situation. She had some good stuff too, plenty of fine acids that would have burned a hole right through her attacker's thick red carapace.

Why did I do this, she thought? *The professor is not going to be happy at all when he finds out. Uggh! I really am a gnit-wit!*

It had all started a few days prior. Gnipper, as usual, had meant well. She had followed the scientific process completely. First, she identified her problem. She wanted one of her favorite cookies—double chocolate butterscotch with raisins. Unfortunately, the cookies were in a nearly impenetrable fortress, completely unassailable by any gnome—the top shelf of the pantry.

She had tried the usual fixes. First she moved over a chair from the kitchen table to stand on, but it wobbled, and as quickly as her feet were both squarely on top of the wooden death trap, it was flinging her to a future filled with a bruised behind and a cookie-less existence.

Seeing that her physical methods had not worked, she tried a more political approach. She sat down and drafted a finely worded letter to the Lord Protector himself, asking for military assistance in her time of need. She didn't need much; a single battalion would do, or even just one ogre of moderate height and enough discipline not to eat her cookie himself.

It had been twenty-seven minutes since the letter went out in the mail and still there was no response. Now she finally understood why people said such hateful things about the government.

Having exhausted all possible avenues, Gnipper decided to turn to the only answer she knew could work—science.

Gnipper was like all gnomes that lived on the island of Rosehaven, a lover of science, academia, and bragging about how much smarter they were than everyone else. Bragging was actually the official pastime of the Gnomish community. It had beat "complaining" and "hide and seek" in a vote at the last meeting.

Unfortunately, being a gnit-wit somewhat took away from those fantastic bragging rights. You see, gnomes loved hats, the bigger the better. They were a status symbol, a way to show the world how much smarter they were than everyone else. This was because a gnome couldn't earn their prestigious, pointed, felt cap, called a *pileus*, until they had somehow created a scientific advancement that benefitted the entire gnomish community.

A young gnome was expected to be able to accomplish this feat by their twelfth birthday. Those who couldn't were branded with the most horrific insult in the gnomish language—*gnit-wit*. Strictly translated, it meant "one without adequate knowledge."

Gnipper was now twelve-and-a-half. She was officially a gnit-wit. It was one of the reasons why she always wore an iron skillet on her head. It was her placeholder. It made her feel like less of a failure, and reminded her that she'd one day earn a real hat.

Gnipper tried to not let the insults bother her, but it was hard, especially when they originated from her father. He was the worst. He had the tallest hat of any gnome in the entire community, and he made sure she heard about it every single day. It was why he changed their last name to Tallhat. He was afraid blind creatures wouldn't be able to *see* how important he was and he didn't want to deprive himself of their respect.

She had really thought this idea was going to be the one that removed her of that horrible gnit-wit nickname. Not only would she be able to get her cookie off the top shelf, but she would also be providing a service to any gnome denied baked goods based on their limited height. It was a riddle that begged to be solved. If she could just make it work, everyone in the community would be rushing to crown her with her pointy new headgear.

She just had to invent a growth serum.

The basics were easy. All she had to do was trick a creature's body into producing the proper growth hormones in sustained bursts, and then shut off when they reached the desired size.

Her preliminary test results showed that she was halfway there. Her test subject, Chloe, the queen of the fire ant farm that she kept in her lab had indeed grown like she had intended. It was the stopping that didn't quite happen as planned.

And that was what brought her to the problem she was in right now. Gnipper had expected the ant to double in size, but the angry, winged creature buzzing in front of her was hundreds of times her original size. She was almost as tall as Gnipper, a whopping two feet and nine inches.

"OK, Chloe," Gnipper said in a calmer voice. "I don't want to have to hurt you, but I'm going to need you to go sit down while I find out exactly what went wrong."

Chloe did not listen. Ants seldom did.

Instead, she swung her stinger violently at her, trying desperately to impale the little pink-haired scientist. A quick backhand from Gnipper with her iron hat-turned-shield grazed the fire ant's backside just enough for the stinger to land a few inches above her head, instead of inside it. The force of the blow sent her sprawling to the ground, where she landed in a heap.

Chloe saw her opportunity. Gnipper was defenseless in front of her.

The angry insect flew back a few feet, ready to initiate another strike, when the creak of the door to Gnipper's lab seemed to distract Chloe.

"Gnip?" drifted in a loud but squeaky voice. "You down there?"

Gnipper's heart began to race. It was the sound of her closest friend in the whole world, well, usually her only friend in the whole world—Samantha Bushytail.

"Sam, help!" Gnipper screamed as loud as she could.

Her friend bounded down the stairs with the speed and grace of a well-trained ballerina.

Gnipper couldn't remember the last time she felt so relieved. If there was anyone in Rosehaven that had the ability, and the willingness, to save her, it was Sam.

Sam was a Florensian, though better known around Rosehaven as a member of the squirrel-kin. They had been a race of humans, trapped thousands of years ago by a powerful demon sorcerer to live out their existence in the bodies of squirrels. Over time, they had become the most fearsome warriors that Rosehaven had ever seen. The best of the best formed the Acorn Guard, a prestigious unit of bodyguards assigned to the Lord Protector himself. Sam's father was the captain, and had trained her since birth to become the first female member of the Guard once she came of age.

Leaping down the stairs, the young squirrel-kin quickly assessed the situation.

As usual, Gnipper couldn't tell what she was thinking. Sam's face was a stoic mask of poise and confidence. Sam quickly reached down toward her belt and drew out the two silver basket-handled rapiers she wore at all times, even while sleeping. The thin metal swords, each a foot long and masterfully sharpened, glinted in the dim sunlight pouring in from the open door at the top of the stairs.

Sam let out a battle cry as she jumped down the last few steps to engage the fire ant. The shrill, piercing chirp-scream immediately got her attention. Chloe spun to meet the new threat.

Sam hit the ground, bending her powerful, black-furred legs as she landed. Her large fluffy tail extended over her back, mirroring the imposing red stinger in front of her. Her swords were tautly held out to each side of her body, ready to strike in the blink of an eye.

The red ant hissed and thrust with its barbed tail, wanting nothing more than to inject the squirrel with its deadly venom.

Sam, as usual, was ready. She sidestepped to the left, the stinger flying past and missing her torso by a few inches. She spun, bringing her left blade down in a quick arc and tearing into the armored carapace of the insect.

Chloe let out a milk-curdling scream. It wasn't quite blood curdling, but still quite scary.

Sam spun around, pivoting on her paws and repositioning herself to the side of the ant's torso. She stabbed viciously with her other blade, doing her best to aim for a vital organ.

Clank!

The blade bounced harmlessly off the thick, armored exoskeleton.

Chloe let out another loud hiss, began to beat her wings, and flew speedily toward the open door of the lab. Sam took another swing, but Chloe had already left her reach.

"Chloe, no!" screamed Gnipper as the ant left the room.

"Gnipper, what did you do?" snapped Sam, momentarily losing the calm demeanor she always tried to maintain.

"I *may* have accidentally given Chloe a serum that would help her grow," Gnipper answered. "On the bright side, it definitely worked."

"Ugh," growled Sam. Her voice showed clear annoyance. "I really just wanted to go to the park today. Maybe have one little normal afternoon. We could have played tag with the fairy kids, or gone fishing with some of the merfolk boys down at the pier, but no. Now we have to spend another afternoon cleaning up one of your messes."

"Yeah," replied Gnipper with a sly smile and a shrug.

"Tell me again why I'm friends with you?" Sam asked, her voice already losing its edge.

Gnipper had no answer. She just walked up to the squirrel-kin and hugged her tightly around the waist.

"Okay, Okay," Sam said after a moment, "I'm not mad. I guess it won't be that bad. It's just one insect. One gigantic, armored, flying, angry, venomous bug that could kill either of us in less than a second."

"Well….," said Gnipper, looking straight up at the ceiling. It was her universal sign that there was more to the truth.

"Gnipper, *please* don't tell me you tested this on *all* the ants in the colony." Sam peered at her wide-eyed.

"Of course not," she replied innocently. "That would have been pretty stupid of me, don't you think?"

"Thank the gods," Sam answered, reflexively looking upwards. "I thought there was going to be more of these things running around today."

"Oh, there is," Gnipper responded. "But not because I infected more. You see, the queen's pregnant. She could lay her eggs at any moment. I'm pretty sure the serum I used will be passed on to her offspring. I did it that way on purpose, so I could see if this would be a generational improvement."

"Oh, Gnip," answered Sam with a sigh. "How many eggs are we talking about? One? Two?"

"Three thousand five hundred," Gnipper answered slowly. "Give or take a few."

Sam closed her eyes and began muttering in fast paced Florensian. She was mad. She only did that that when Gnipper did something *really* bad. Gnipper had asked her once what she was saying, and she just told her that she was "asking her mother for patience."

Having lost her mother as well, Gnipper understood the need to ask for some divine guidance every now and then.

"It's not an exact number," Gnipper interjected, trying to make her friend feel better. "It's just an estimate. It could be a few less."

"That doesn't help," Sam responded. "What can we do to stop it?"

"I was thinking about that while Chloe was trying to kill me. I think I can make a counter-agent to the growth serum. It won't shrink Chloe, but it will stop her from having anymore giant babies. If we can get the serum into the eggs before they hatch, it should also stunt their development and make sure the eggs hatch at a more normal size."

"Wouldn't it be easier to kill her and destroy the eggs?"

"We can't do that!" Gnipper cried. She was completely offended.

"Umm...why not?" Sam asked.

"Because it's not Chloe's fault this happened. She doesn't deserve to die."

"Gnipper, she's a bug." Sam gave Gnipper her are-you–serious look as she spoke.

"So...she's still a living thing," Gnipper responded. "She deserves a chance to live her life."

"So your plan is to create an experimental antidote, find Chloe, give it to her and all 3,500 of her eggs, and then leave a fifty pound insect to live out its days in peace?"

"No, that would be stupid." Gnipper chuckled at the idea.

"Good," Sam said, a slight smile returning to her face. "I thought you were thinking a bit crazy today."

17

"Nope," Gnipper said. "We just have to relocate her to a place where she can't hurt anyone, and no one can hurt her."

"*Oh good*," said Sam sarcastically, "I was afraid your plan would be difficult."

"It shouldn't be that hard, Sam. We just need to fly her to one of the islands off the coast. Once Chloe's there she'll burrow into the ground to start her colony and eventually lose her wings. She can live her days as queen as she was intended."

"So we fly her there?" Sam asked skeptically. "On her back, I'm guessing? And how do you plan on us getting back here to Rosehaven?"

"I've already thought about that. We need to see Gnanny Gnogglebottom."

Sam looked at her and rolled her eyes. "Gnip, that was the last thing I wanted you to say."

It took the girls almost an hour to reach Gnanny Gnogglebottom's cottage. She lived far outside Rosehaven's protective walls. It was at least a half mile away from any other creatures on the island.

Gnanny's cottage was a peculiar blend of colors, and for lack of a better word, garbage. The entire area surrounding the small stone building was filled with old, half-melted metals, piles of colored rocks, and bright, patched-together quilts flown on flagpoles.

Gnanny, like all gnomes, loved dedicating her life to science and discovery. Her field of choice, however, was quite different from anyone else. Some gnomes even said it wasn't science at all, but Gnanny would just argue with them until they got so confused that they just agreed with her.

You see, she was the island's foremost expert in expressionist art. Gnipper, like most of the gnomish community, didn't actually have a clue what expressionist art was, but she did know that her Gnanny loved anything that involved creating. She was always sculpting, drawing, quilting, and making ceramics, among other things. She was constantly experimenting with new forms and ideas and showing off strange work that everyone agreed was "riveting." Gnipper realized at an early age that gnomes called art "riveting" when they refused to admit that they had no idea if it was good or not.

Gnanny had earned her pileus at the age of five, after inventing a new form of artistic expression known now as finer painting. No one on their governing body, the Board of Knowledgeable Gnomes, had known if her work was actually deserving of the award or not. But not knowing anything about art themselves, they were all afraid to call it bad and be wrong about it. Gnanny always laughed when she told that story, and she always said, "It amazes me how much gets done when people are too afraid of sounding ignorant to say no."

Gnipper walked past a large copper statue of a centaur riding atop an oversized wheel and knocked on the door.

No one answered, though both girls could hear a low grunting sound coming from inside.

"Do you hear that, Sam?" Gnipper asked with concern. "It sounds like she's in trouble."

Pushing Gnipper out of the way, Sam spun and forced her powerful right leg into the center of the door. It cracked, fell of the hinges, and landed in front of them.

"You know Sam, I don't think it was locked," Gnipper said, but the eager squirrel-kin had already entered the house and was looking around.

The first room was almost bare, except for dozens of wooden cuckoo clocks hanging from the walls. Though each one showed a different time, they all came together with loud, rhythmic tick-tocking.

"It's time for you to die!" bellowed a deep baritone voice.

"Aaaahhhhhhhhh!" A grunting scream ricocheted off the walls in response.

"Second floor!" yelled Sam, bounding up the old wooden staircase as she drew her swords. Gnipper followed as closely behind as her little legs allowed, reaching the top a few seconds later.

Gnipper gasped at what she saw. Gnanny stood with her back to them, clutching a large metal-handled axe high above her head.

"I'm sorry," Gnanny said, "but it looks like it's time for you to *split!* The old gnome bellowed out a maniacal laugh, "*Hahahahahaha!*"

"Gnanny, no!" screamed Gnipper, but she was too late. The white-haired old gnome had already swung. As the axe reached its prey, the target's body shattered, spraying moisture and sharp remnants into the air. Gnipper flinched as shards hit her in the face. She had never expected blood to be so cold and pointy.

"Gnippy, my little nugget!" exclaimed Gnanny as she lowered the axe and turned to greet them. "What are you doing here?"

Gnanny stepped away from her kill, dropping the axe on the ground as she opened her arms to hug Gnipper. Gnanny was very large for a gnome, especially in the width department.

She had hair died several different colors, unable to decide on just one, that mingled with her natural gray highlights. Over her paint-stained dress was an even more paint-stained blue smock. Her pileus, once white, was also spattered with color, and unlike the rest of the hats in the community, it had a brim.. Gnanny said it was to protect her skin from the evil sun, but Gnipper always thought it was because she liked to be different. In all, Gnanny looked like a bright, happy rainbow, and that was how she liked it.

"Gnanny," Gnipper asked in a panic, "why are you killing someone?"

"Killing someone?" she answered with confusion in her voice. "No, no nothing like that. I'm making an ice sculpture. See?"

She stepped to her left to reveal a half carved block of ice. Once Gnipper realized that the artwork was intended to be a goblin with a severe lack of pants, she quickly averted her eyes.

"But what about all the voices we heard," Sam interjected, "and yelling about it being time for someone to die?"

"Oh, that. I was just rehearsing a play I wrote. It's a new genre. I call it a *murder mystery*. I'm thinking about pairing it with a nice dinner. In case the idea doesn't catch on, at least people will get a nice meal and can leave happy. What about you two? Why are you here? Not that I'm upset that you came to visit your old Gnanny, I just figured on a nice day like today, you'd be at the park causing trouble and breaking some boys' hearts."

"Gnanny!" said Gnipper as her cheeks reddened to a shade that matched her rose pink hair.

"Now Gnippy, don't be shy. Your father may have changed your name to Tallhat, but you'll always be a Gnogglebottom, and no male can resist a Gnogglebottom, trust me on that one. How is my son the professor these days anyway? As usual, I never hear from him—no letters, no visits, nothing."

"He's good, Gnanny," Gnipper answered as she inspected the ice sculpture. "He works a lot."

"Always was a hard worker, that son of mine," Gnanny said. "A big jerk, but always a jerk who worked hard."

"Yeah, that pretty much sums him up," quipped Sam somewhat under her breath.

"Well Gnanny, the reason we're here is simple. I need your help."

"What did you do this time?" Gnanny responded with feigned grandmotherly strictness.

"Well," started Gnipper, "to make a long story short, I administered a growth serum to a very pregnant and angry fire ant queen named Chloe, who promptly escaped from my lab and is now possibly giving birth to an unstoppable insect army of doom."

"Oh good," said Gnanny Gnogglebottom with a smile. "I was afraid it would be something we couldn't handle. I assume you already have a plan worked out? You are my granddaughter after all, I would expect nothing less."

"I was thinking that I could administer an anti-serum to shut off the growth spurts in the eggs, and then we would just have to relocate Chloe. We could bring her to one of the small islands off the eastern coast."

"And you would need me to use *Amelia* to come pick you up?"

"Who's Amelia?" asked Sam.

"Not *who*, Samantha, *what*. *Amelia* is one of my greatest inventions. She's a flying machine made out of nothing but lumber, quilts, and heat. It's taken me all over this planet. Not on purpose mind, you…it's just very tough to steer."

"Yes, Gnanny," replied Gnipper. "If you could pick us up and bring us back, that would be fantastic. It's all we need you to do."

"No," she replied calmly, shaking her head from side to side.

"No? Why not?" asked Gnipper confused.

"Because I'm not letting my only granddaughter risk her life for such a crazy plan," Gnanny paused for a moment, "at least not without me. This sounds like far too much fun to miss out on!"

"Fine Gnanny, but no telling the professor."

Gnanny Gnogglebottom laughed, "That's always my first rule as well!"

****

Working together at her lab, Gnipper, Gnanny, and Sam were able to create the anti-serum within a few hours, but as they walked south out of the city they realized that a few hours had been far too long.

Directly in front of them was a sixty-foot tall funnel shaped mound of dirt. Chloe had already begun a nest for her colony.

"Seems like we don't have much time," said Gnanny. "We need to find an entrance into that monstrosity before anyone from the city watch gets here and tries to take the situation into their own hands. We could really have an emergency if we have to deal with those idiots as well."

"West side," replied Samantha with confidence. "About a hundred yards from our current position."

"Ah, the eyes of the young," responded Gnanny with a twinge of jealousy in her voice. "These days, with my eyes, I'm happy if I go an entire afternoon without walking into a wall. Lead on."

As they reached the entrance to the ant mountain. Darkness completely engulfed the tunnel. Gnipper reached into her knapsack and took out a torch, lit it, and held it in front of her.

The walls seemed solid, though they were not much taller than she was. She and Gnanny would be okay, but Sam was going to have to duck. She wasn't going to like that.

"Follow me, girls," said Gnanny as she took the torch from Gnipper, "and don't worry. There is absolutely no reason to feel *ANT*sy."

Oh no, thought Gnipper, *not the puns*.

If there was anything in the world Gnanny loved more than her art, it was making puns. Horrible, unnecessary, improperly timed puns. For a few seconds Gnipper thought about turning back. Surely, seeing the whole city slaughtered by rampaging insects wasn't nearly as bad as listening to Gnanny make jokes all afternoon.

"Stop," whispered Sam suddenly. "I think I hear something."

"What is it?" Gnipper whispered back.

"It could be nothing. I'm not sure. It sounds a bit like scurrying."

At the edge of the light, Gnipper could see movement. "Over there," she whispered pointing at the area.

Two large red ants walked into view.

"Oh no," whispered Gnipper. "Soldier ants! That means the eggs have started hatching."

Sam drew her swords.

"No, don't attack," Gnipper warned. "I have an idea."

Gnipper quickly ripped off her knapsack and began to rummage around in it as the two soldier ants approached.

"You might want to hurry up a bit, Gnippy. Those two seem a little *ANT*isocial."

Gnipper groaned from the pain of the pun but continued searching her bag.

"Got it!" she exclaimed, raising a small vial. She uncorked it, poured some on her hand and began covering herself with it.

"What is it?" Sam asked.

"Perfume made from Chloe's pheromones. Now we should smell like one of her colony. Ants don't have ears and they don't see well, so they determine friends and foes via smell. And now we smell like a friend!"

"Positively f*ANT*astic, Gnippy!"

"Gnanny, please stop with the puns!"

"Oh Gnippy, I'm just trying to lighten the mood. If you can't have fun when you exterminate giant insects, then when can you have fun?"

"Let's just see if it works," Sam said skeptically. "When does anything I make not work?" said Gnipper. "If anything, it works *too* well. Just to be safe, make sure you're ready to defend us if something goes wrong."

"I'm always ready," Sam replied, annoyed at the insinuation that she might not be prepared for that situation.

Gnipper stepped towards the ants, the vibration of her feet against the ground drawing their attention. They approached her as she stood still, her heart pounding in anticipation.

The antennas on both ants were vibrating wildly as they moved their heads up and down over the little pink-headed gnome, trying to figure out what, exactly, she was. After a few tense moments, they continued on, smelling Gnanny and Sam in the same manner before continuing towards the edge of the tunnel.

"Well done, Gnippy!" cheered Gnanny. "It seems that, for the moment, we can pass as ants!"

"Yeah, but if the eggs have already hatched Gnanny, then we need a new plan."

"Gnip," said Sam. "I think we might have to think about blowing up the nest."

"I packed explosives!" offered Gnanny excitedly.

"No, we can't do that," she responded emphatically. "We just need to get all the ants off the main island so that there won't be any way for them to harm us."

"And how do you expect us to do that?" Sam asked sternly.

"Sleep!" interrupted Gnanny.

"There's no time for that, Gnanny," Gnipper snapped back. "This is serious."

"No, Gnippy. I wasn't asking for a nap. I was suggesting we put them to sleep. Once they are out we can ferry them over to their new home and clip their wings so they can't fly back. Then we let the dock master know to restrict access to that particular island, not that anyone ever goes to the uninhabited ones anyway."

"Gnanny, that's perfect," Gnipper said with a big smile. "I have plenty of ingestible anesthetic from when I did exploratory surgery on Fuzzy."

"How is that pet rat of yours?" asked Gnanny.

"Much better now," Gnipper responded. "Turns out he just had gas. Anyway, while I get the sleep aid, Sam can explore the rest of the nest, find out how many eggs hatched and apply the anti-serum to those that haven't. While we do this, you go home and get *Amelia* and a long piece of rope. We'll meet near the entrance, sprinkle their food supply with the anesthetic, put the little ants down for a nap, string them together, and fly them to their happy new home. Easy as pie!"

"*Yeah*, sounds really easy," griped Sam. "You're not the one risking your life in the deadly ant nest."

"Oh, Sammy," said Gnanny. "You're right. It's not fair of us to ask you to do something so dangerous. No one can expect such insane bravery from such a young rodent. Perhaps we could have asked this of you if you were older or if you had just been born a boy…"

"Give me the anti-serum!" Sam snapped. Gnipper smiled. Gnanny had figured out real quick how to motivate Sam. Just insult her bravery or her gender and she'd do pretty much anything you wanted.

"How long does this pheromone last?" Sam asked as she did a quick final check of her supplies.

"Oh, I have no idea," Gnipper responded. "Never tested it before today."

"Wonderful," Sam grumbled. "I'll meet you at the entrance when I'm done."

Both gnomes offered Samantha Bushytail luck as she disappeared into the dark recesses of the ant nest.

****

The house was quiet when Gnipper returned. Her father was still at Thales Academy. He *was* headmaster, as he liked to remind Gnipper. Fuzzy was taking a nap in her laboratory. Trying not to disturb him, she collected all the materials she needed: a large container of anesthesia, a dropper to put it in their food, and a cookie out of the backup jar on the kitchen table—double chocolate butterscotch with raisins, her favorite.

When she arrived back at the nest, she saw that neither Gnanny nor Sam had returned. Gnanny she figured would take a while, she had farther to walk and she was quite slow, even for an elderly gnome. Gnipper liked to describe Gnanny's gait as that of an obese duck with gout.

Sam's lack of appearance concerned her more. She was anything but slow and it shouldn't have taken very long to sprinkle the anti-serum on the eggs.

"Chahahlalalalala!"

It was the unmistakable battle cry of the squirrel-kin, a series of squeaks and chirps that drove fear straight into the hearts of their enemies. Or made them laugh. Either way, they were always distracted.

"Oh good," thought Gnipper, "here she comes."

A few moments later, Sam somersaulted backward out of the entrance tunnel, her weapons drawn and blood dripping from a wound in her right leg. Are you alright, Sam?!" Gnipper asked with shock and concern in her voice.

"I think so. Stinger just grazed me." Sam spoke through gritted teeth, the pain obviously greater than she was letting on.

"Pheromones must have worn off," Gnipper said unnecessarily.

"You think?!"

"Yeah, or else they wouldn't have been able to detect that you weren't an ant."

"I was being sarcastic, Gnip!" Sam growled at her.

"Oh...sarcasm confuses me."

"Be ready," Sam commanded, ignoring Gnipper's response. "Here they come."

Two large, angry soldier ants came rushing out of the tunnel, heading straight for Sam. They looked like the same two that had smelled them earlier, but Gnipper couldn't be sure. They all seemed to look alike. Gnipper hoped that wasn't speciesist of her.

Preparing for the onslaught, Gnipper grabbed the handle of her skillet and pulled it off of her head. She swung it violently back and forth in front of her, ignoring the fact that the ants were still twenty yards away.

Sam took several steps back, placing herself in between the approaching ants and her very un-athletic friend.

The attackers lunged forward, closing the gap between them and the squirrel-kin. Gnipper watched nervously as Sam swiped back and forth at the ants, trying to keep them at bay. They struck back, violently thrusting with their stingers as Sam parried one and barely dodged the other. Normally, Sam could have fought them off for hours, her energy levels were often inexhaustible; but today was far from normal. The leg wound was clearly slowing her down, and the loss of blood seemed to be making her a bit woozy. Gnipper even saw her almost lose her footing twice, something that was unimaginable for her agile friend. Gnipper needed a plan and she needed one fast or else they were both about to become ant food.

Gnipper wracked her huge gnomish brain for an idea. She thought about all the hours she had spent studying her ant farm, the observations, and the experiments... and the ANTENNAE!

"Sam, don't attack the body!" Gnipper screamed. "Go for the antenna!"

Sam listened without question, feinting a thrust with one hand while swiping across the top of the ant's head with the other. Her sharp blades sliced through the dangling appendages with ease. The exoskeleton was not nearly as thick at those points.

The ants let out a piercing howl of pain. Gnipper shuddered.

She felt horribly guilty. If it wasn't for her mistake, those innocent insects wouldn't have had to endure such pain. She felt like a terrible gnome.

"What did that just do?" asked Sam, as the ants began to mindlessly wander away.

"Antennae are their main sensory organ," Gnipper responded sadly. "It would be like you losing hearing, touch, and smell at the same time, while already having the sight of a mole."

"So they don't know we're still here?" Sam asked.

"That's a positive statement," Gnipper said, trying not to get choked up over her decision.

"Good, Gnip," replied Sam with a renewed vigor, "because here come a whole lot more of those things."

Sam wasn't lying. At least twenty more ants were pouring out of the nest. Gnipper wondered if they were responding to the screams of their mutilated brothers.

"We need to go, Gnip! Now!"

"I will not be posing any counterargument to your plan," Gnipper replied.

"I said, I agree with you!"

"Good," Sam blurted out, as she turned to run. "Follow me."

Sam turned back toward town with Gnipper following at her heels. With Sam's injury slowing her down, Gnipper found that she was able to keep up with her furry-tailed friend for the first time in her life. Despite her joy, this was not a good thing. It meant they were both running very slowly.

The ants had picked up their scent and had taken to the air to follow them. They quickly gained on the two fleeing girls. The terrifying buzz of their wings was just inches behind Gnipper's head. She pushed her little legs to go faster, but evolution had not built gnomes for running. They were thinkers, teachers, and scientists, along with other careers that didn't ever involve physical exertion.

"Gnippy? You look like you need some help!"

The soft yell of her Gnanny's voice carried from far above her. Her lungs ready to explode, Gnipper looked up and saw hope in the form of a huge, round, floating ball of quilts. Gnanny Gnogglebottom rode in a large wicker basket chair suspended from the bottom. Hanging below the flying machine was a knotted rope quickly flying toward them.

"Gnipper, the rope!" Sam said excitedly.

Had she had any breath left at all, the sight of the rope would have made her chuckle. She couldn't climb a rope that was stationary, and yet Gnanny wanted her to jump up, grab it, and climb while it moved higher into the air and ants were flying around trying to attack her. It was absurd just thinking about it.

Gnipper watched as Sam sped up, trying her best to ignore the pain in her leg. She put away her blades, leaped toward the rope with two outstretched paws, and grabbed onto it. The squirrel-kin's momentum took her and the rope flying directly away from Gnipper. While it sailed towards its peak Sam yanked herself up a few feet, leaned back, and flung her legs in the air. Flipping upside down, she grabbed the rope with her feet and wrapped her two powerful lower paws around a sturdy knot.

Gnipper realized her plan.

Shifting her weight in the opposite direction, the now upside-down squirrel opened up her arms as she flew out of control back towards Gnipper.

Gnipper closed her eyes and hoped for the best.

Sam grabbed her by the two thin straps of her horribly stained white overalls, lifting her into the air just as a stinger flew centimeters under her foot.

"Don't drop me!" Gnipper screamed as she dared to open her eyes.

"I wasn't planning on it!" Sam retorted. "But you're going to need to fight them off; my hands are busy making sure you live through this."

A small drop of blood rolled off Sam's thigh and into Gnipper's face. She tried desperately to spit it out. *"Phhhhh."*

"Gnipper! Pay attention, here comes one!"

"I'm trying to pay attention," she yelled back. "Stop bleeding on me!"

Though the balloon was gaining altitude quickly, not all the ants had given up their pursuit. Three were flying toward the two girls hanging helplessly in mid-air.

"Uh, Sam...what do I do?" Gnipper asked, trying to mask the fear in her voice.

"Hit them with something," Sam replied, as if the answer should have been obvious.

Gnipper grasped the skillet from her head and swung it as hard as she could at the closest ant as it attempted to close its mandible around her foot. She missed by a few feet, but it was enough to make the ant back off for a moment.

Another one came in from underneath, farther than Gnipper could reach with her skillet. As his head snapped toward her body, she kicked down and her little leather boot landed directly in his eye. She could hear a light snap and the insect began to drop down toward the ground, trying to gain his bearings.

ground. He got up, but seemed too stunned to follow them again.

Her victory lasted only a moment as the first ant was back, snapping at her heels. She decided that the time to worry about how terrible of a gnome she was for hurting innocent creatures was long gone. They lost her sympathy the third time they tried to kill her. That was always her rule. She could overlook two murder attempts, but after the third, anything was fair game.

"I need momentum!" Gnipper cried out.

"Who's Momentum?" Sam asked back, confused.

"Spin me!" Gnipper replied with authority.

Sam flung all her weight to one side, sending the two girls into a quick spin. Using her momentum to cooperate with her strength, Gnipper swung the skillet with every ounce of her being.

It was approximately one ounce more than she was able to hold on to.

The skillet flew from her hands awkwardly, but their angle still put it on a path with her target. The pan-turned-projectile slammed into the side of the ant's head, crunching his skull and sending him hurtling back towards the ground as a slimy green liquid oozed from the wound.

The third ant, aware of the failure of his brothers, rapidly turned back toward the nest.

"Gnip, you did it!" Sam screamed with elation.

"I wish I didn't have too. I hate killing things, even bugs."

"You didn't Gnip, look."

Gnipper looked down below them as the two ants that had dropped from the sky very slowly moved back to the colony.

"Their exoskeletons must have saved them," Gnipper commented.

"Yup, though I bet they're not going to feel too great for a very long time."

"At least they'll be feeling something," Gnipper said, feeling relieved.

"There's their food supply. It's right next to that secondary entrance. I found it before when I was inside."

"Gnanny!" Gnipper yelled up. "Find us a good place to land!"

*****

It took several hours to make sure all the ants were out cold, tied up well, and shuttled back and forth between the main land and the small island Gnanny chose as their landing site. It gave them plenty of time to bandage Sam's wound while they waited.

"Well, looks like it's time to head back," Gnipper said as she clipped the final pair of wings. "They should be waking up in a few minutes, and they will be *very* unhappy. I'm going to miss you, Chloe," she said to her former pet as she rubbed her head just between her two twitching antennae.

"C'mon, Gnippy," Gnanny said as she prepared *Amelia* for launch. "Let's get you two home before the professor notices you're missing. Unless you want me make a stop somewhere of course?"

"Where would we stop?" Gnipper asked curiously.

"I don't know…" Gnanny said with a big smile, "I was thinking maybe *ANT*arctica?"

"Gnanny!" cried Gnipper, trying hard not to smile back. "Thanks."

Want More Rosehaven? Check out these fine stories:

Rise of the Retics (Rosehaven Book 1)
Return of the Fae-blood (Rosehaven Book 2)

Gnit-Wit Gnipper and the Perilous Plague
Gnit-Wit Gnipper and the Ferocious Fire-Ants
Gnit-Wit Gnipper and the Devious Dragon

Sir Dudley Tinklebutton and the Dragon's Lair
Sir Dudley Tinklebutton and the Sword of Cowardice
Sir Dudley Tinklebutton and the Unholy Grail

T.J. Lantz is from York, Pa where he was an elementary school teacher. He currently lives in the Caribbean nation of Grenada with his wife Maya, who is studying to be a Veterinarian, his daughters Arya and Piper, and his three dogs. He enjoys dreaming about the day he gets to return to America and escape the giant island insects that want to kill him.

Ana Santo is a freelance illustrator who has recently left the science field to follow her dream of being an artist. She is currently working on multiple graphic novel projects.

Made in the USA
Middletown, DE
14 December 2017